For Carson and all the Saffers
JH

For Bud
RC

Tyrone O'Saurus had a dream.

It was not the dream his father had for him.

My son, the dentist.

Tyrone did not want to be a dentist.

It was not the dream his mother had for him.
"You are so smart," she said. "You would be an
excellent lawyer."

Tyrone did not want to be a lawyer. His legs were too
wiggly and jiggly to have to sit at a desk all day.

"You are quick on your feet," his brother, Johnny, said.
"You should try out for American football. You could
be team captain. Like me. Win lots of trophies. Like me.
Play in the DAFL someday. Like me."
Tyrone did not want to play in the Dinosaur American
Football League someday. That was not his dream.

"My arms are too short to throw," he said.

"That hasn't stopped me," his brother replied. "You have to
dream big and work to make your dream come true. Like—"

"You," Tyrone said. *Maybe*, he thought, *I should give up my
dream and be an American football star instead. Like Johnny.*

"I'll try," said Tyrone.

"Go for it!" Johnny said.

Well, the kid can move, but he sure can't throw.

Or catch.

Tyrone got stronger.

But he didn't get better.

No matter how hard he worked, Tyrone knew he would never be as good at American football as Johnny.

Then he saw the strongest dinosaur he had ever seen.

"Excuse me," Tyrone said. "You are so strong. Do you play American football?"

"Me? Oh, no!" the strong
dinosaur said.

"You're very tall. Do you play basketball?"
Tyrone asked.

"Goodness, no," she said. "I'm working out so I can be a stronger dancer."

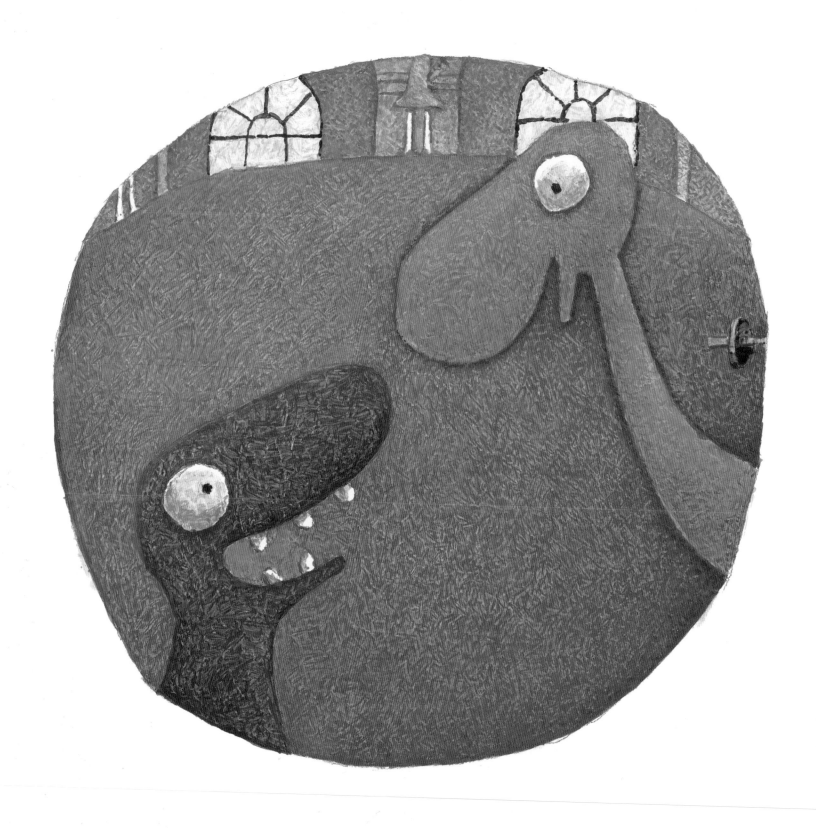

Tyrone could not believe his ears. "You're a dancer?"
he gasped. "Dancing is *my* dream," he said softly.

"That's your dream?" Johnny asked. "To dance?"
"Well," said Tyrone, "I guess, I mean, it sort of ... is..."

"If that's your dream," Johnny said, "you have to go for it!"

"Really, Johnny?" said Tyrone.

"Really, Tyrone," said Johnny.

"I'm Brontorina," said the strong dinosaur. "And these are my friends. We are learning to dance at Madame Lucille's Outdoor Dance Academy for Girls and Boys and Dinosaurs and Cows. Come with us, Tyrone."

"I would love to, Brontorina," Tyrone said.

And off they went.

"This is Tyrone," Brontorina told Madame Lucille. "He wants to learn to dance."

"Welcome, Tyrone!" said Madame Lucille. "Music, Magnolia!"

"You are a very good – and very strong – dancer!"
Madame Lucille told Tyrone.

"Do you really think so?" asked Tyrone.

"I do!" said Madame Lucille. "Would you like to study with us? You will need to work hard, but there could be a very special part for you in our next dance show."

"Oh, I will work very hard," said Tyrone. "Thank you, Madame Lucille!"

When it came time for the dance show, no one cheered louder than Tyrone's family.

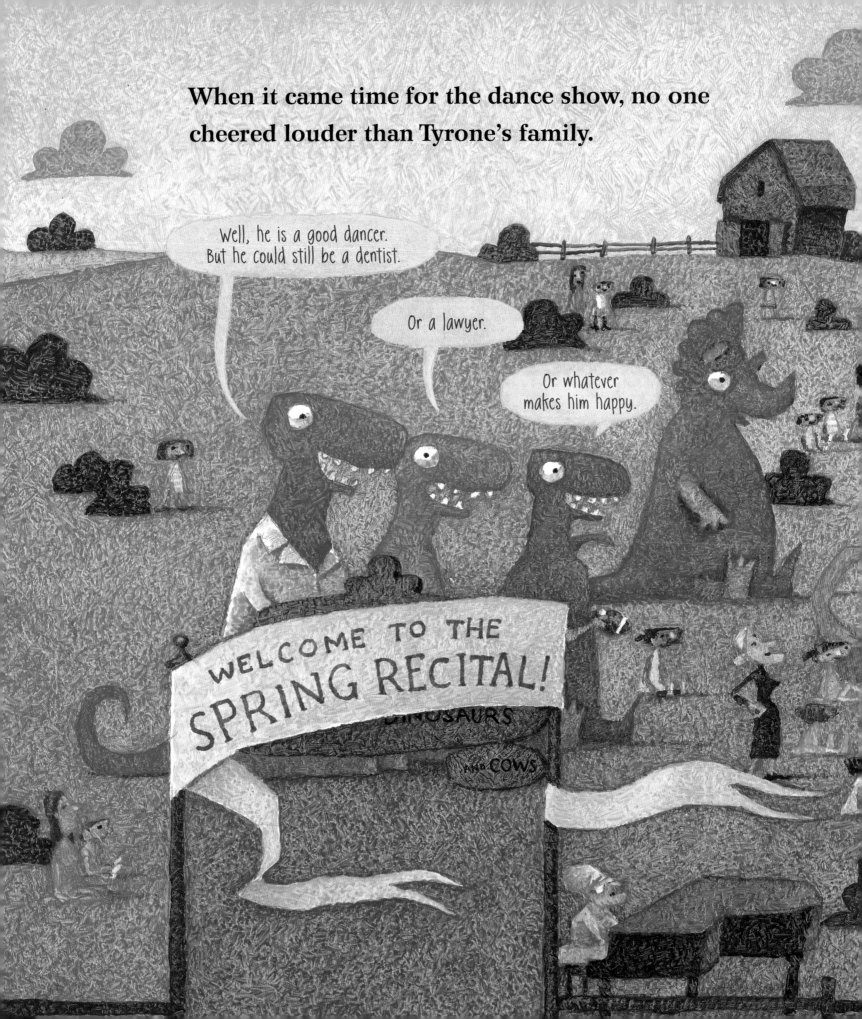

Tyrone was so happy, he thought his heart would burst. He knew he would always be happy as long as he could dance.

And it all began with a dream.